John Mitchinson

Charge Delivered in St. Michael's Cathedral, Bridgetown,

Barbados

John Mitchinson

Charge Delivered in St. Michael's Cathedral, Bridgetown, Barbados

ISBN/EAN: 9783337403355

Printed in Europe, USA, Canada, Australia, Japan

Cover: Foto ©Andreas Hilbeck / pixelio.de

More available books at **www.hansebooks.com**

CHARGE

DELIVERED IN

ST. MICHAEL'S CATHEDRAL, BRIDGETOWN, BARBADOS,

BY THE RIGHT REV.

JOHN MITCHINSON, D.C.L., D.D.

BISHOP OF BARBADOS AND THE WINDWARD ISLANDS ;
FELLOW OF PEMBROKE COLLEGE, OXFORD ;
HONORARY CANON OF CANTERBURY CATHEDRAL ;

At his Second Visitation of his Diocese,

ON

THE FESTIVAL OF ST. JOHN THE EVANGELIST, 1878,

Being the Sixth Year of his Consecration.

From the Author.

Oxford and London:
JAMES PARKER AND CO.
1879.

SUMMARY OF CONTENTS.

APOLOGY for a quinquennial Visitation.

The events of the period in the World and the Church.

The Eastern War, and the attitude of the English Clergy.

The New Court, and its failure.

The Ridsdale Judgment: even if faulty, entitled to obedience.

The Confession agitation: Confraternities: the true position of Confession in the Anglican System.

The growth, wide-spread and aggressive intolerance of unbelief.

Study of recent evidential literature its best antidote, and sound and clear dogmatic teaching its best prophylactic to the young.—Scientific and philosophic hypotheses not to be taken for proved facts on authority.

Necessity of study, and suspended judgment on Church controversies of the day, e.g. Inspiration and Eschatology.

Approximation to the Anglican Obedience of bodies yearning for reform in France and Spain, as well as Old Catholics, Armenians, and other Eastern Christians.—Bolder and sounder attitude of the American Church towards Haiti and Mexico.—Divergence from the English Church of Nonconformists, especially Wesleyans: possibility of re-union on the basis of mutual independence of system, but defect of orders remedied.—Analogy of Friars in the Mediæval Church.

The Lambeth Conference: non-publication of debates.—The questions of the Barbados Church Council, how brought before the Conference: replies of the Conference on the Province of the West Indies, the extension of the Diaconate, and Moravian Inter-communion. — Second Conference of West Indian Bishops, and their advice.—Proposed Co-adjutorship to the Bishop of Antigua.

Events in Barbados.—The troubles of 1876.—Fruitless attempt at general re-consideration of methods, rectified by ruri-decanal meetings of clergy.—Re-construction and division of the old collapsed Diocese of Barbados.—Changes in the clergy-staff of Barbados.—Principle of administration of patronage defended.

A Charge, &c.

NEARLY five years have elapsed since I last formally visited my Diocese, and addressed you in the Charge which usually accompanies such periodic inspections, though you have had many opportunities since my Primary Charge of learning my sentiments on the passing topics of Church interest, in the form of Addresses to my Church Council, and in Pastoral Letters to you from time to time.

Five years exceeds the interval canonically fixed for episcopal visitations. It could not well, however, in this instance have been otherwise; for one of those years, 1876, has by tacit consent in Barbados been suffered to drop out of the calendar of Church-work, while for six months of 1878 I have myself been absent from my Diocese.

They have been five eventful years both to the world and to the Church.. This is not the time or place to speak of that sanguinary war which, by its hardly paralleled atrocities, perpetrated on both sides with a fiendish rivalry in savagery, has imprinted an indelible bar-sinister on the escutcheon of modern European civilization. Suffice it to remark on this, that since the thirty years' war, which was in its character essentially a religious war, no war in modern times has so entirely reproduced the phenomena, and kindled the impetuous passions of the Crusades, whether in the combatants or in the on-lookers. It has been astonishing and painful to note how a large section of the English clergy, comprising great and justly-honoured names, blinded, as it would seem, by strong pseudo-Christian sympathies with one of the combatants, forgot that attitude of self-continence in matters political, which best beseems the officers of a kingdom not of this

world ; and, most improperly in my judgment, endea-
voured to control and overrule the foreign policy of
the responsible Ministers of our Sovereign ; emulating
thereby that attitude, so justly censured, of the Roman
Catholic hierarchy in Ireland, (but more excusable in
them, as being avowedly an *Imperium in Imperio*,) of
constant and arbitrary interference in the general politics
of the nation.   Nothing, surely, is more calculated to bring
the Church into discredit, and to give reality to the foolish
bugbear of "clericalism," than this attempt at usurpation
on the part of the clergy of functions and an influence
not legitimately their own.

These five years will be memorable in the history of
our Church at large for the culmination of the growth
of ultra-ritualism, and for the energetic, though, as it
would seem, abortive attempt made by the bishops and
the legislature to repress it.   That attempt took form in
the Public Worship Regulation Act, which was passed
with such singular unanimity of political parties, and the
creation of the new Court, which was attempted to be
floated into general confidence by sailing under the colours
of the ancient Provincial Courts of Canterbury and York.
Rightly or wrongly, the Court has failed to obtain the
confidence, or anything like the cordial acquiescence, of
many even of those whose excesses would not bring them
within the scope of its jurisdiction.   And though we may
deplore this, and feel that some coercive authority must
be recognized as final and entitled to prompt submission,
we cannot entirely marvel at it, bearing in mind the
jealousy which all Churchmen, whether lay or clerical,
naturally and properly feel at any encroachment, whether
real or apparent, on the part of Cæsar on the things of
God, and any attempt to abridge or alienate those powers
of jurisdiction and correction, which they deem to be the
inalienable duty and prerogative of the spiritual power.
It was certainly to be regretted that the Act in question
was passed so entirely without concert or consultation
with the spiritualty, even without eliciting any formal
expression of opinion from that body which claims to

represent the order chiefly concerned. For, I suppose, none of us bishops are weak enough to believe that we are regarded by our brethren of the other orders of the clergy as in any sense their mouth-piece or their representatives.

The Court, however, has entirely failed to restrain the admitted evil of clerical lawlessness; and, whether from the novelty of its procedure, unregulated as it is thus far by usage and precedent, or from other causes, has hitherto effected little but miscarriage of justice, and collision with other jurisdictions.

Another most important event of the period has been the Ridsdale Judgment, which was looked forward to with eager anxiety, as a deliberate and final revision of the Purchas Judgment, which was felt to be incomplete and unsatisfactory, as having been given in an undefended suit.

This Judgment, as you well know, had for its scope the settlement of the ritual of the Eucharist. Its two main points of general interest were the prohibition of what are called the Eucharistic vestments, and the virtual recognition of the Eastward position at consecration of the elements as legal. Probably, this was substantially the settlement of the long-vexed question which most moderate men, uncommitted to the exaggerated intolerance of either party, would have desiderated, as an equitable compromise, at once securing to the Sacrament its due meed of reverence, and yet clearly differencing it from the Roman Mass. And yet we may reasonably regret that this Eastward position, which seems so permissible a construction (to say the least of it) of the rubric before the Consecration Prayer, should have been legalized in what many may deem an ungracious and left-handed way, leaving it virtually open to unsettlement in any parish where an aggrieved parishioner (or, more probably, non-parishioner) may complain that he fails to see the manual acts, (as though these were in any sense essential to the due consecration of the elements). We may regret, too, that the prohibition of

vestments is made to depend on the interpretation and
virtual abrogation of the Ornaments' Rubric (which, you
will remember, was re-cast and adopted as part of the
statute-law of the land, by King, Lords, and Commons,
at the last revision), by what must always grate harshly
on constitutional ears, an injunction of a Tudor Sovereign.

All this is ground for legitimate regret; matter for
free discussion, for free criticism; for in a free country and
in a free church, just as we refuse to recognize infallible
authority in any ecclesiastical person or synod, so we
refuse to credit any tribunal, however august, with free-
dom from error and perchance unconscious prejudice.
Criticism, I say, is natural, lawful, even wholesome, so
it overstep not the limits of criticism, and demean itself
by imputing corrupt motives.   More than this, it is the
indefeasible right of the defeated party to seek by all
constitutional means a rectification of the law which has
been interpreted to their disadvantage; to move Convo-
cation and Parliament to relax restrictions, or to re-cast
in their interest and render clearer rubrics, the plain sense
of which they may deem to have been obscured by judi-
cial decisions.   But nothing, in my judgment, can excuse
disobedience to the law as laid down by the highest court
of the Church and realm.   Its decisions may be unsound,
may be unjust in the opinion of those whom they affect:
still, they are the final award of the final court, which, according to the present settlement of Church and State in
England, has the right finally to decide controversies; and,
reasonable or unreasonable, they ought to be promptly,
literally, and loyally obeyed.   There are, of course, occa-
sions when resistance to the powers that be is a matter
of moral and religious obligation; but it behoves all who
take upon themselves this most grave responsibility, to
be fully persuaded in their own mind that morality and
religion demand and justify an attitude which is, on the
face of it, so manifestly repugnant to the Word of God.

Among the other incidents of the period we must reckon
the outburst of popular indignation which assailed the
Society of the Holy Cross, when that most ill-judged

and mischievous Manual of Confession, which had the sanction of their authority, was brought by Lord Redesdale before the notice of Parliament. May I be permitted to express my doubts, in passing, whether such confraternities are either expedient or wholesome in the Christian Church; whether they do not rather tend to obscure and weaken the sense of the great brotherhood of the Church Universal, and the more restricted, but perhaps more consciously realized, brotherhood of each Christian's particular or national Church, as well as those lesser brotherhoods which bind the faithful together in love and in good works, viz. the Diocese and the Parish. I am not blind to the value of organization and association for the purpose of achieving this or that special object, for the better discharge of this or that special duty to the members of Christ's Body; but where there is no such special extrospective scope, it appears to me that the principle of confraternities militates against the full realization of the fundamental doctrines of the one Catholic and Apostolic Church, and of the Communion of Saints, by substituting a more special, self-regarding, self-regulated obligation for the more general.

That outburst of indignation was, like all other popular clamours, indiscriminate and unreasoning. It has not, however, been without its use to the Church, in winnowing and sifting opinion, and in directing the attention of many of her loosely-thinking children to the actual position which Confession holds in her system, and to the limits within which it must be worked. In answer to the violent and sweeping denunciations of all confession of sin to a human guide, it is sufficient to say, that the craving for this as a spiritual discipline and aid is too deeply seated in certain types of human nature for any religious system to afford to neglect, ignore, or repress it. But, like other impulses, it requires to be regulated. The principle which the Church of England adopts in clear contradistinction to Rome is this, Confession in her system is a medicine of the soul. In the Roman system, Confession is its necessary food. With them it is essential to the worthy reception of the Eucharist; it becomes part of the regular routine of religious life, and increases in frequency, the higher the standard of spirituality which is attained. With us it is an exceptional mode of dealing with soul-disease, a lower, not a higher state: it is compulsory on none, even on the soul-sick: it is evidently contemplated as a remedy and alleviation, to which rare or, at least, exceptional and unhabitual recourse should be had. I know not how the teaching of the Church of England on this subject, as fairly gathered from her formularies, can be more clearly given than in the words of the Anglican Episcopate recently assembled at Lambeth:—"No minister of the Church is authorized to require from those who may resort to him to open their grief a particular or detailed enumeration of all their sins, or to require private confession previous to receiving the Holy Communion, or to enjoin, or even encourage, the practice of habitual confession to a Priest, or to teach that such practice of habitual confession, or the being subject to what has been termed the direction of a Priest, is a condition of attaining to the highest spiritual life. At the same time, they are not to be understood as desiring to limit in any way the provision made in the Book of Common Prayer for the relief of troubled consciences."

But even a more important and more ominous feature in the religious history of these five years, has been the marked advance and more unreserved outspokenness of unbelief: more ominous, because it is easier for the excess of belief, i.e. credulity and superstition, than for the defect, to gravitate back to the mean. If it was found at Lambeth to be practically impossible for a strong Committee, aided by the lucid sagacity of the Bishops of Killaloe and Gloucester, to put forth any report on this momentous question that could satisfactorily handle it; it stands to reason that I, who have neither the range of reading nor yet the mental acumen necessary for such a task, am utterly unequal to so doing in a Visitation Charge. Without, however, attempting to particularize, much less to discuss, the many forms and gradations of non-belief, I may usefully draw your attention to one or two points in connection with it. First, its universality and its multiform character. It is not too much to say that it pervades literature: it is no longer the apparent logical tendency of a certain school of biologists: I do not think it is an exaggeration to say, that you seldom meet with a treatise, or even a paper, in our more thoughtful and philosophic periodical literature, which deals with cosmic or psychic phenomena, or problems, which does not more or less argue on some hypothesis of self-causation or self-evolution. Secondly, its aggressiveness. It is no longer a demand for equal toleration with belief and orthodoxy, for candid recognition of the co-ordinate but divergent lines of religion and philosophy, of faith and reason. Agnostic and materialistic philosophy has dropped the defensive attitude, and carried the war into the very camp of faith. It gives no quarter. Its almost savage intolerance (if I may without impropriety so describe it), and its impatience of dissent from the dicta of its favourite prophets, if it were not ominous as regards the future outlook, would be grotesquely amusing.

You may perhaps expect me, my reverend brethren, to indicate to you where you are to look for answers to these attacks, not on Christianity alone, but on Religion ; for refutations of the many forms of Atheism and Scepticism which, we cannot doubt, must have come in the way, and undermined or imperilled the faith, of the reading or thinking members of your flocks. I confess myself entirely unable to do so. It is impossible that there can be anything like discussion, with the hope of agreement, between systems which have no common ground, and which, in fact, mutually exclude each other. I do not even recommend you to study and endeavour to master the vast sea of materialistic and sceptic literature with which the press now teems. I recommend to you rather the constructive method, of studying and mastering the foundations on which your own Christian faith and, in fact, religion generally are based, not resting content with the excellent manuals and standard books on Evidences of a century ago, but keeping yourselves well abreast of the evidential literature of the Church of our day, which, God be thanked, is clear, full, able, and accessible to all.

One other consideration, or rather caution, I would advise you to impress on the sceptically disposed, or on those who, as they grow up, are likely to fall within range of temptation from this quarter. Do not be misled by the authority of great names into accepting their dicta as proved conclusions of Science or Philosophy. This is a very real danger, and the source of much mischief both to religion and to science. The exclusive appeal to authority is dangerous in religion, where the enlightened reason is an important factor in the attainment and acceptance even of revealed truth, (" I speak as to wise men," says St. Paul; "judge ye what I say"). In science it is little short of treasonable, and calculated to subvert the very *raison d'être* of science. And when we add to this danger of accepting scientific and philosophic conclusions simply and solely on the authority of the great prophets of science and philosophy, the fact that these prophets have not been careful (I put it most modestly and most guardedly) to keep a clear line of demarcation between what is inductively proved, or even inductively highly probable, and what is mere brilliant hypothesis, ingenious, strikingly probable, little short of an intuition or inspiration if you will, but still mere undemonstrated hypothesis, you will see the necessity for the caution I have given you, not to be misled by the authority of great names into accepting speculations as though they were incontrovertible truths.

I have advocated the study of evidential literature on your own part, let me also advise you to endeavour to secure, not the study of Evidences, (for to most young minds this, like all ratiocinative study, is more or less distasteful and unfruitful, though there are exceptions,) but clear, sound, intelligent, dogmatic teaching in all the articles of the Christian Faith, as well as in the distinctive principles, history and credentials of our mother Church of England on the part of the younger members of your flocks. And here I speak not so much (or at least by no

means exclusively or preeminently) of the children in our
elementary schools, as of the young persons of both sexes
of our upper and middle classes in society. Ignorance, or
at least haziness, as to what they believe and why they
believe, is, I am convinced, a fatally common predisposing
nidus for the malaria of scepticism to germinate in, on the
principle that the empty house (as the parable teaches)
invites the tenancy of the seven spirits more wicked than
the first.

A clergyman, now-a-days, needs to find or make leisure
for study, if he would keep abreast of the controversies
within the Church, as well as with her outside warfare.
Many beliefs which we have come to regard as settled
theological dogmas—the precise foundation and bearings
of which have perhaps never been exhaustively pursued or
authoritatively and explicitly defined, because never seriously called in question—have in our feverish age of enquiry
and speculation been arraigned and thrown into the cru-
cible of investigation. And there is no doubt that the
general sense and teaching of the Church will, as time
goes on, be found to have been considerably modified
by such discussions, without the least fear of imperilling
thereby the sacred deposit of the faith once for all delivered to the saints, which is the very palladium of the
Church's existence. I may mention two such controversies, as illustrations of my meaning: the controversy
on the meaning, nature and limits of Inspiration, and the
controversy which is at present so deeply engrossing
thoughtful minds in the mother Church on what is called
Eschatology, i.e. the condition of the life beyond the grave.
In recommending you to read and ponder on the literature
of these controverted subjects—such books, for example,
as Canon Farrar's "Eternal Hope," and the thoughtful
discussions and criticisms which it has evoked—I am far
from counselling you rashly to discard cherished opinions
and convictions, recommended and hallowed by the un-
questioned acceptance of some of God's truest saints;
I am still further from counselling you, yea, I rather earn-
· estly dissuade you, from rashly and needlessly unsettling

the belief (so inextricably intertwined with conduct) of your several flocks: but I do counsel you to careful, dispassionate reflection on these topics in your own study; I do dissuade you from unenquiring, unreflective condemnation of opinions, which by their novelty may startle and, perhaps, shock you as you first meet them; and I venture to propound to you as a sound principle of action in the study of religious controversy, never to be more dogmatic than the Church of which you are ministers, and to be ever cautious of hasty limitation of terms which the Church has not authoritatively defined.

The controversies of recent years have led me into a digression. Let me return to the events of general interest to the Church. No one can fail to have been struck by the tendency towards approximation to the Anglican Communion in one or other of its great centres, the Churches of England and of America, on the part of communities of anxious minds yearning for greater purity of faith and practice, in the midst of corruption and degradation and ignorance. Christians seeking a purer faith, and yet clinging tight to Apostolic order and Catholic tradition, seem to have recognized the Anglican obedience as a natural *point d'appui*. And such I cannot doubt that, by God's merciful Providence, it is destined to be, whether in our generation or in the far-off future. You are all sufficiently aware of the *rapprochement* which has taken place between the old Catholics of Germany and ourselves, and have read of the presence and active participation of English Divines in their conferences. It would be premature to speculate whether this is destined to lead to more organic theological union, or simply to more unrestricted fraternal sympathy; as, indeed, it would be premature to forecast the future of this great movement (the most important since the sixteenth century) from within the Church of Rome towards reformation of doctrine and discipline. You may not, however, be aware that overtures for assistance, whether towards securing for their postulants for orders better instruction in the faith, or towards obtaining an apostolical ministry to supply the means of grace, from which, through their attitude of antagonism to Rome's corruptions, they are debarred, have been made, and were discussed at Lambeth, from Spain and France, as well as from the Armenians and others in the far East. The American Church has already listened to such overtures from Haiti, and has consecrated a Bishop of the negro race (whose friendship it was my privilege to form at the Conference) to nurse up a native Church, destined to be an independent branch of the Anglican Communion as soon as its tutelage is ended, and it can safely stand alone. She is already entertaining similar overtures, and has resolved on similar action, in the case of Mexico. I cannot help sympathizing with the greater boldness, in such emergencies, of our American sister, and wishing that we were equally prompt and equally helpful. I am well aware that to encourage or create a schism in the Church, even though that Church be corrupt, is a grave responsibility, and is at best an unsisterly act. I am fully alive, too, to the much greater soundness of self-evolved reform, which was happily our own good fortune when we rebelled against Roman usurpation. But how is reform to be self-evolved; how is a ministry to be perpetuated; how are the means of grace (the very life-blood of every religious movement) to be secured, when there is no such spontaneous national unanimity reformwards, as there was in our case, and when, without the grace of orders conferred *ab extra* from some Apostolic source, the reforming movement must die, or must forfeit its Catholicity, with all that that involves? The heads of our English branch of the Communion, seem to me to incur a grave responsibility to Christendom in temporising in such cases, and dashing high hopes with good advice and mere words of sympathy, and to be unintentionally subserving the cause either of Rome or Non-Catholicism. Surely the American Church is sounder-judging : heresy and schism are both terrible evils, but of them it would seem that schism is the least.

On the other hand, it must be regretfully admitted, that there appears to have been within the period a growing divergence from the English Church on the part

of Protestant nonconformity. Whatever may have been
the cause, whether it be the decay of what is commonly styled Evangelicalism in the Church, and the
growth and rapid development of a party, the apparent
sympathies of which are with Rome more than with Pro-
testantism ; or whether it be the craving for religious
equality as the natural and logical outcome of religious
toleration, combined with a growing impatience of anything like a dominant Church, with exclusive prerogatives,
and a social prestige closely connected with its position as
an establishment,—no thoughtful observer can be blind
to the fact that the attitude of dissent has, within quite
recent times, passed from that of rivalry (not incompatible with sympathy and even friendship) into undis-
guised hostility. .

Most markedly is this change of attitude towards the
Church observable in the Wesleyan body. Till recently,
that body of separatists from us (alas that they should
have drifted into a relation so alien to the avowed
principles and intentions of their pious founder!) recognized a tacit and informal alliance with the Church in
England, especially on the subjects of religious education and State establishment. On both these points it
will be found that the Wesleyan front is now entirely
changed. The disruption of this alliance is the more to
be regretted, when we consider the history of the great
Wesleyan movement, its general identity on all essentials
of doctrine with ourselves, its ardent spirit of missionary
enterprise, and, we may add, the abundant measure of
success with which these efforts appear to have been
sealed by the Holy Ghost. What good Churchman can
have failed to thank God that so much good has thus been
wrought, even though it may seem to have been in antagonism to us, and in curtailment of our own progress ?
And yet, on the other hand, what good Churchman can
have failed to deplore recent separation—symptoms though
they be but trifling in themselves—such, for example, as
the assumption of the term *Church*, to denote alike the
Wesleyan community as an organization and body cor-

porate, and its several places of worship, as well as of
the conventional courtesy title of *Reverend* for its ministers; a courtesy which we all of us right willingly
accord as a mark of personal respect, and which most
of us deplore was ever made a matter of litigation, but
which, if it is taken to imply more than a respectful de-
signation of men who for their work's sake are justly
worthy to be revered, lies beyond the province of any
law-court to confer, and would on our part be an act of
disloyalty to the principles of our Catholic and Apostolic
branch of the Church to recognize.

But one cannot help feeling that the time has now
come, or cannot be far off, when great religious organiza-
tions like the Church of England and the Wesleyans, to
say nothing of other and, perhaps, more divergent bodies
of Christians, should through their respective leaders
enter into serious discussion, not on their points of agreement which are confessedly numerous, and embrace all
essentials of the Christian Faith, but on the points which
hold them asunder, to see if some honourable *concordat* may
not be arrived at ; not fusion, not absorption, nothing that
will violate the organization or traditions of either—but
which will enable the ministers of both to work side by
side on terms of reciprocity, and of mutual aid and intercourse in the great work of evangelization, each in
their respective lines, and according to their several uses,
—no longer as rivals, much less as enemies, but as mutually helpful allies in a common army, under the one
great Captain of our salvation.

I cannot but think that the great, and now apparently
hopeless, divergence which keeps them asunder, would be
found to be the question of a valid and regular ministry ;
and by mutual conference, surely the essentials to validity
of orders and conferring of mission might be agreed on,
and shortcomings (if shortcomings there be in this respect) remedied, with no violence done to any cherished
Nonconformist sentiment of independence of the shackles
of establishment and Acts of Uniformity, and with full
liberty to develope according to their own inherent life.

The existence within the unreformed Church of the Middle Ages, of the minor religious orders, or Friars, demonstrates the possibility of the co-existence of settled diocesan and parochial arrangements, with evangelistic efforts on the part of these free-lances, as we may call them, of Christendom, independent alike of Episcopal jurisdiction and parochial autonomy, and subject only to their respective generals or provincials; and seems to indicate an analogy which the post-Reformation Church would do well to follow, and thus gather into one focus all the rays, however apparently many-coloured, of religious zeal and missionary effort, so as to present an united, although not necessarily uniform front, to the great enemies of that one religion they all ardently profess, viz., unbelief and godlessness at home, and heathenism or (as we deem them) false, or partially false, religious systems abroad.   Looked at from the very lowest and most utilitarian point of view, episcopal ordination, transmitted through the unbroken channels of either the Anglo-Colonial, the American, or the Irish Church, could not possibly render the ministrations of the Wesleyan, or other dissenting preacher or missionary, less efficacious to those who now value them; and it would render them efficacious, as regards the ministry of the Word and Sacraments, to those who cannot conscientiously now so esteem them, but who often irregularly, and with more or less latent sense of inconsistency, now resort to them.

Among the most important events of general interest to the Church during the period must be reckoned the Lambeth Episcopal Conference.   One hundred bishops from the most distant parts of the world, and representing Anglican Christendom under its most varied aspects, assembled under the presidency of the Primate of Canterbury.   With two exceptions, the entire bench of English bishops attended, not indeed continuously, but with more or less regularity throughout the session; the entire Scottish Episcopate was there; nine out of twelve of the Irish prelates; eighteen from the Protestant Epis-

copal Church of the United States of America; while
the Ecclesiastical Provinces of Canada, Rupertsland, South
Africa, Australia, New Zealand, and India, were more or
less largely represented; five out of the six West Indian
bishops were there; so that our section of the Church
had its full weight in the deliberations of the Conference.
Many of you doubtless have regretted, as did some of
ourselves, that beyond the formal issue of the adopted
reports of Committees, with a few words by way of pre-
face and conclusion, no authentic report was suffered to
transpire of the discussions of each day. It is undoubtedly
matter for regret that so many weighty, and really elo-
quent addresses, on some of the most important and interesting topics that can occupy a Churchman's thoughts,
should have been practically lost to the Church, or at
least to the Church of to-day, and that the record of
them should be consigned to virtual oblivion among the
archives of Lambeth library. Few who were present could
fail to regret this, particularly in reference to the really
brilliant debate which took place on the different aspects
of infidelity, a debate which, to us who had the privilege
of listening to it, was in itself more than compensation
for a voyage to England and back.

It may be in your recollection that the Church Council
of Barbados addressed me before my departure to England, and requested me, if opportunity were afforded of
discussing such matters at the Conference, to endeavour
to obtain some expression of opinion on the establishment (if possible) of a Provincial Synod in this portion
of the Colonial Empire, and on the advisability of admitting to the Diaconate men who might at the same
time pursue some honourable secular calling.

Manifestly, the topics suggested fell naturally under
the sixth proposed subject for discussion, viz., the condition, progress and needs of the various branches of
the Anglican communion. On the day, therefore, allotted
to the discussion of that subject, I anxiously waited for
an opportunity of bringing these questions before my
brethren. The morning sitting was long and interest-

ing, bearing upon the history of the Cumminsite schism, and the relations of the Anglican Church to the so-called Reformed Episcopal Church and its *soi-disant* episcopate, the fruits of that needless and most unhappy secession.   The afternoon sitting was occupied with interesting statements and debates, having reference to the present attitude and needs of the Irish and Scottish Episcopal Churches.   Time wore on, and it became evident that the day's debate must close without an opportunity being accorded of pressing any of the problems and difficulties of the Colonial Church : I knew many Colonial bishops were circumstanced similarly to myself.   I therefore rose, and after pointing out to the Conference how I was circumstanced, and reading to it from your address the instructions with which I was entrusted by my Diocese, I moved that as it was patently impossible in the short hour still remaining before the closure of the first session of the Conference to discuss, or even to hear the different needs and difficulties of the Colonial Church, a Committee should be appointed to receive, during the fortnight's recess, questions submitted to them in writing by Bishops desiring the advice of the Conference on difficulties or problems they have met with in their several dioceses, and to report thereon to the Conference when it resumed its sittings.   This was seconded by the Archbishop of York, and I had the satisfaction of a strong and sufficiently representative Committee being named, to deal not only with my own questions, but with those of other bishops, both English and Colonial.

The Committee was composed as follows :—

Archbishop of Canterbury, *Chairman.*	Bishop of Manchester.
	Bishop of St. David's.
Archbishop of Dublin [a].	Bishop of Kingston.
Bishop of New York.	Bishop of Antigua.
Bishop of Barbados.	Bishop of Rupertsland.
Bishop of Chichester.	

[a] The Archbishop of Dublin did not attend the sittings of the Committee.

I submitted to it the following questions :—

I. On Provincial Organization.

1. Assuming a group of dioceses to desire to be combined into a Province, what steps should they take?

2. If difficulties lie either temporarily or permanently in the way of a Representative Provincial Synod, can the bishops of the Province alone form a Provincial Synod?

3. If so, ought their authority as a Synod to be restricted, and, if restricted, to what extent and in what directions, on the score that they are not strictly representative of the dioceses which form the Province?

4. Does the Conference advise the creation of a metropolitical see, or that a primate be elected from and by the bishops of the Province, or that the senior bishop for the time being should be Metropolitan?

5. Whence is the Metropolitan to derive his mission as such?

II. On the Diaconate.

1. May a diocese, if its circumstances, in the judgment of its Synod or of its bishops, should require it, resolve to modify the generally-received status of the office of Deacon in the following directions :—

(*a.*) By recognizing it as practically as well as theoretically a distinct order of the Ministry, no more necessarily leading on to the priesthood than the priesthood does to the episcopate.

(*b.*) By admitting to the Diaconate laymen of any age (over twenty-three), who are following any calling not inconsistent with the Ministerial character or with Ministerial usefulness, without calling them from that vocation, or imposing any restriction on the full discharge of that vocation.

(*c.*) By dropping the title of *Reverend* from the Diaconate, and confining it to the presbyterate; styling the deacon simply *Deacon So and So*, and by dispensing with customary clerical attire in the case of the deacon, except when performing Ministerial duties.

2. If the Conference should deem this, or any of it, lawful and not in itself inexpedient,—

(*a.*) Ought the above-sketched system to apply to *all* deacons, or simply to those who do not contemplate seeking the higher degree?

(*b.*) What examination (beyond strict enquiry into life and conversation) should such deacons be required to pass?

(*c.*) Ought exception to be made as regards intellectual tests in favour of any persons, e.g., graduates of Universities, or men advanced in life, or where it is not intended to seek or give licence to preach?

(*d.*) Should such deacons ever be advanced to the presbyterate without abandoning their secular calling *as a source of emolument*, and "giving themselves wholly to it?"

3. What limitations (if any) should a diocese assume in availing itself of this relaxation (if allowed), in reference to the Diaconate?

I also proposed a series of questions having reference to the attitude of the Anglican Church towards Moravian ministers, especially in these West Indian Islands.

The special questions submitted by me were :—

1. If a Moravian presbyter, or deacon, desires to be received into the Anglican ministry, ought I to (*a*) ordain him absolutely; (*b*) re-ordain him conditionally; (*c*) accept his orders as valid, and simply give him mission in the Anglican Church?

2. Can I canonically and regularly commission a Bishop of the *Unitas Fratrum* in my Diocese, either to confirm or to ordain for me, or to do both episcopal acts, according to the Anglican ritual?

3. Am I justified in consenting, if called on, to confirm children, or ordain presbyters or deacons, or to do both, for the Moravians, in their churches, and according to their ritual?

4. May Anglican presbyters and deacons, with their Bishop's sanction, officiate and minister the Sacraments in Moravian churches according to their ritual, and invite Moravian presbyters or deacons to execute the functions

appertaining to their office in Anglican churches, and according to Anglican ritual?

These questions received the careful consideration of the Committee, and the report on them severally was thus finally adopted by the Conference :—

"With respect to the West Indian Dioceses, assuming such Dioceses to desire to be combined into a Province, we advise that the formal consent of the Diocesan Representative Synods, if free (as regards their relation to the State) to give such consent, be first obtained.

"The Bishops of the several Dioceses would then forward such formal consent, or expressed desire, to the Archbishop of Canterbury, requesting him to give his sanction to the formation of the Province.

"Whether the General Synod of the Province should consist of the Bishops, with representatives of the clergy and laity of the respective Dioceses, or should consist of the Bishops of the Province only; and, in the latter case, what limitation should be imposed on the powers of such purely Episcopal Synod, is a question which ought to be left to the Diocesan Synods to decide, with the approval of the Archbishop of Canterbury.

"If the West Indian Dioceses be formed into a Province, it seems desirable that a Metropolitan should be, in the first instance, elected from and by the Bishops of the West Indian Dioceses.

"The questions submitted respecting the peculiar circumstances of the West Indian Diaconate appear, upon full consideration, to be such as can be adequately decided only in Diocesan or Provincial Synods.

"With regard to the questions now raised respecting Moravian Orders, we recommend that the Archbishops of England and Ireland, with the Bishop of London, the Primus of the Scottish Episcopal Church, and the Presiding Bishop of the Protestant Episcopal Church in the United States of America, the Bishop superintending the congregations of the same upon the Continent of Europe, and the Bishop of Gibraltar, associating with themselves such learned persons as they may deem emi-

nently qualified to assist them, by their knowledge of
the historical difficulties involved, be requested to advise
thereon as circumstances may require."

On the first point, viz. the formation of a West Indian
Province, the advice of the Conference seemed so explicit,
that those members of the West Indian Episcopate who
were present at the Conference, resolved, as soon as its
sittings were finally closed, to hold a second Conference
of West Indian bishops in London, to mature matters, if
possible, for the speedy formation of the Province, and
the invitation of the several Diocesan Synods to incor-
porate themselves in it.

Under the presidency of the venerable Bishop of Guiana,
now the father of the British and Colonial Episcopate, the
Bishops of Kingston, Antigua, the Falkland Islands, Barbados, and Nassau, met, and discussed the scheme of provincial organization. We agreed to a joint address to
each Synod and Church Council in the West Indies, in-
viting their several consent to be united with the rest in
a Province of the West Indies ; and we further request
a distinct utterance on the part of each such Body as to
whether it is their wish that the Provincial Synod should,
at least for the present, and until the different dioceses
have otherwise resolved, consist of the Bishops of the
Province only.

We felt, however, that the golden opportunity of mutual conference as to details should not be lost; and
though, technically speaking, we ought to have simply
put before you all these two questions, and waited for
your several replies, we could not afford to forego a discussion among ourselves of the details of the scheme which,
in principle, we hoped you would, with pretty general unanimity, adopt. We, therefore, agreed (prematurely, I grant,
but I think wisely, and economically as to time) on the general scheme of a Province, constructed on the hypothesis
of a solely Episcopal Synod ; and this scheme, along with
the two questions which I have already read to you, it
will be my duty to lay in full before you, my reverend
brethren, and the lay representatives in Church Council

to-day, and before the several Church Councils of the Windward Diocese during my approaching visitation tour, and to obtain from you severally a definite reply in the affirmative, or otherwise, which I may forward, with as little delay as possible, through the Bishop of Guiana to the Archbishop of Canterbury.

It may have appeared to you that the reply of the Conference on the two other topics, the Diaconate, and our relations with Moravians, was vague and unsatisfactory. Permit me to point out the real value of the opinion elicited in either case.

In my opening address to the present Church Council, written on my voyage to England, and forwarded too late for its actual purpose of an opening to your Session, but printed for your general information in the "West Indian," I wrote as follows, in reference to the extension of the Diaconate, or rather its restoration to its primitive theory as a semi-lay order : " It would not be according to ecclesiastical order for such a step as this, practically useful though it obviously would be, to be taken without the consensus of sister dioceses, and (probably) the approval of the collective Anglican Church." The answer of the Conference practically waives any such right of approval on the part of the Church at large ; it definitely remits it for settlement to Diocesan and Provincial Synods, and thus removes an obstacle in the way of a prompt and early settlement of the question. It treats the question, in fact, as one of those which (as the thirty-fourth Article declares) "every particular or national Church hath authority to ordain, change, or abolish, so that all things be done to edifying."

With regard to Moravian intercommunion, I do not think a wiser decision could have been arrived at. I neither expected nor desired a direct and dogmatic answer from the Conference, and my own wishes are exactly met by what the Conference has counselled. Questions of intercommunion between Churches are not mere matter of sentiment, to be widened or restricted by the enthusiasm or jealousy of a majority, as either may happen to be dominant. No Church, possessing, as ours does, the priceless heirloom (so carefully, I may even say pro-videntially guarded, in evil days of carelessness) of an undoubted Apostolical descent, and of undoubtedly valid ministrations on the part of its three Orders, is justified in hastily complimenting this away, even from the best of all motives, brotherly charity. And the ques-tion of the historical descent of the Moravian ministry is, as the Conference admits, complicated with some his-torical difficulties. But this is the very reason why, in the interests of brotherly charity, we should dispassion-ately study and seek to solve these difficulties ; and I know of no body of men to whom this solution may be more confidently entrusted, than the above-mentioned prelates, in association with learned theologians. It is to me a matter of thankfulness, that the question of full intercommunion with a body of Christians (towards whom, in these dioceses, my sympathies have been so warmly drawn), upon the principle of co-ordinate ecclesiastical organization, and of organic unity without uniformity, seems now nearer authoritative settlement than it has ever heretofore been.

Before I leave the consideration of extra-diocesan af-fairs, I am anxious to lay before you a matter on which I shall also have to consult the Church Councils of my two dioceses, and request of them a definite expression of approval or disapproval. I refer to the negotiations which have taken place between me and the Bishop of Antigua, relative to his retirement from active diocesan work, and my becoming his coadjutor. The position of affairs is briefly this. The Bishop, as you are well aware, is advancing in years : he has held his most laborious see since 1860, and as all who know him well acknowledge, has never spared himself. In addition to increasing years, the burden of seriously-impaired health is now laid upon him, and his tenure of life, if he remains at his post in the West Indies, has been pronounced on competent authority to be very precarious. On the other hand, with his death or resignation, his entire salary of £2,000 a-year from the

Consolidated Fund, absolutely lapses. Hitherto, he has made strenuous efforts to raise an endowment-fund, but, beyond a munificent contribution of his own towards it, has made but little way towards raising what will entitle him to claim conditional grants from S. P. G., S. P. C. K., and the Colonial Bishoprics' Fund. It is at once to relieve him of the heavy strain on his impaired physical powers, and to ease his mind of the pressure of anxiety at the apparent prospect of leaving behind him a permanently vacant episcopal chair, that I have offered, subject to the consent of my dioceses, and of the legislature of this colony, of which I am a salaried public servant, to undertake the coadjutorship of the Bishop of Antigua during his life, if my own life and tenure of office should last so long. The terms of the arrangement are as follows: he, with the permission of the Crown, and of the episcopal referees of Antigua diocese, will retire from the active administration of the diocese, and reside in England on half his salary, where he will still be able to render good service, by securing a more regular clergy-supply; and will devote the remaining half, viz. £1,000 a-year, towards the endowment-fund of the Bishopric of Antigua: I, in the meantime, undertaking personally to visit his diocese once every two years, or oftener, if any special emergency necessitates my personal presence, and otherwise administering the diocese with the assistance of Archdeacons Branch and Gibbs. The conditions on which I propose to do this are precisely those on which I now visit the Windward Islands diocese, viz. that the Church-people of each island visited should defray the entire expenses of my visit to them. My Windward diocese, indeed, is the only one which will have cause to complain of the proposed arrangement, as they henceforth will have to take turns with the diocese of Antigua in a biennial, instead of annual, visitation. With the help, however, of my two Archdeacons, Laborde and Webb, in that diocese, I have no fear of Church-life there at all stagnating, owing to my less frequent personal presence among them. So far as Barbados is concerned, I doubt whether my coadjutorship will involve any longer absence from this diocese than I now habitually make, which, I need not point out to you, is very far below the six months which the law allows me annually for the visitation of the islands formerly belonging to the diocese of Barbados. The only difference will be, what I myself shall feel in a largely-increased island correspondence, and in the multiplication of anxieties and annoyances ; for these are, I suppose, inseparable from the episcopal office, and increase in direct proportion to the extent of episcopal jurisdiction. But you may perhaps still be disposed to ask, how will this arrangement advantage the diocese of Barbados ? I reply, in the first place, it is a sisterly act for a more favoured diocese to stretch out a helping hand to one less happily circumstanced, just as my offer is simply a fraternal act of kindness from a younger to an elder brother ; and consequently, one in which self-advantage finds no place. It will, however, advantage this diocese, and, in particular, my successors in this episcopal chair, that Antigua diocese should be provided with a bishop of its own, and should not devolve, as it undoubtedly will, unless permanently endowed, on the friendly, unpaid ministrations of future bishops of this see. I am satisfied, therefore, that in undertaking this additional duty while I am still comparatively young, and able to do hard work, I am relieving this see of a prospective incubus ; and should Bishop Jackson's and my life be prolonged for some years to come, I shall be relieved (when he goes to his rest) of heavy duties elsewhere, at a time when I too am becoming more unfitted by age to perform them efficiently, and shall then be able to hand over Antigua diocese to a bishop of its own, presumably in the full vigour of life, with an assured, though it may be limited, income.

I said in the outset of my Charge, that these had been five eventful years to the world and to the Church at large. They have been so in our little world and Church in these islands.

I touch but lightly on the disastrous events of 1876 in Barbados and Tobago. In Barbados, where they were associated with serious political complications, we are still too much within their range to form a dispassionate judgment on them, and the sores are still too recent to admit of any but the most tender handling. I simply allude to them to express my thankfulness, and at the same time my surprise, that apparently they have left but such slight scars on our Church-life. I had certainly feared a long alienation of flock from pastor, as the result of animosities then so disastrously aroused, and of old prejudices rekindled, and a marked diminution of religious influence in consequence. Neither result, to any perceptible extent, appears to have followed; and, I repeat, that it is so is a ground of sincere thankfulness to God on the part of every good man among us, that that great social upheaval has, on the whole, so little disturbed our religious equilibrium.

Towards the close of 1876, feeling that those sad troubles and disappointments might be useful to us clergy in turning our attention to faults or defects in our religious teaching, or in our methods of bringing the sense of religious obligation home to our people, I called all my clergy together, with a view to dispassionately considering our several systems in the light of recent failure, to taking unreserved counsel as to our methods, and, if need be, agreeing on altered lines in which to administer religious instruction and discipline. I found, however, that the time for calm reflection had not yet arrived, that discussion would be unfruitful, and ran some risk of passing into angry recrimination; so I abandoned the attempt till calmer times should come. It is a matter, therefore, of sincere gratification to me to find that during my absence my Rural Deans have acted on the extended authority I some time ago gave them, to summon the clergy only of their several deaneries into clerical chapter, and have commenced a series of such gatherings for the free interchange of clerical experience, and for the discussion of topics bearing on the welfare of the Church in this diocese. Clerical isolation and want of united effort have been serious hindrances to our Church-life here. It is

cheering to think, that this step towards united effort (if
only it be vigorously worked, and not suffered to die a
natural death) has been spontaneously taken.

When I held my primary visitation early in 1874, I was
simply consecrated and commissioned to be the bishop
of the Anglican Church in the colony of Barbados, with
power given by the act which regulated my salary and
status to undertake, if invited, the episcopal charge of the
other islands which had made up the old diocese of Barbados.   Tobago had then formally invited me to do so,
and I had consented ; and Grenada and St. Vincent were
already negotiating.   Eventually all four islands invited
my supervision, and my commission was enlarged in
each instance by a supplementary commission from the
Archbishop of Canterbury.   This, however, constituted a
merely personal union, which on my death or resignation
would be at once dissolved, and the same cumbrous pro-
cess would have had to be repeated on each fresh appointment to the bishopric of Barbados.   In my first charge,
therefore, which I addressed to those several islands, I
advocated formal separation by Royal Warrant from the
old legally-constituted diocese of Barbados, (for it had
never been legally dissolved, and had simply fallen to
pieces from the failure of the Crown to act as regards further appointments to the old see by letters patent), and
combination into a separate diocese by such authority as
we could find to replace the old authority of the Crown
as Supreme Governor of the Church, viz. that of the
Archbishop of Canterbury, the tacitly-recognized Patri-
arch of Anglican Christendom, at least within the British
Empire.   This was agreed to by the several Church Councils, and St. Vincent, Grenada, and Tobago[b] were thus
lawfully incorporated into a diocese of the Windward
Islands, to be always governed, until further order lawfully

---

[b] St. Lucia is not incorporated in this diocese.   It is by Royal Warrant
separated from Barbados.   It now simply consists of two Protestant congregations, voluntarily supervised by the Bishop of Barbados, in the same way
as Continental Chaplaincies in Europe are by the Bishop of London, but
without any clearly-defined jurisdiction.

be taken, by the Bishop of Barbados for the time being. This new diocese is formed upon the principle of what is termed "the consensual pact." On this principle of mutual agreement, as elicited by the resolutions of the several Church Councils, St. George's Church in Kingstown, St. Vincent, has been constituted the Cathedral of the Diocese, with a Chapter of six honorary Canons associated with the Bishops as their Dean ; the diocese has been divided into two archdeaconries,—a necessary arrangement, if their functions were to be real and not merely nominal ; and provision has been made for the assembling of a representative synod of clergy and laity, which will shortly meet me to legislate in Church-matters for the diocese, in every government of which the State-made laws affecting the Church have been repealed by disestablishment.

Several changes in the "personnel" of this diocese have taken place since my last Visitation. Bishop Henry Hutton Parry, formerly Bishop-coadjutor of this Diocese and Archdeacon of Barbados, has been translated to the Bishopric of Perth in Western Australia, where he has been cordially welcomed ; and although domestic bereavement (in which we all sympathize with him) has befallen him in his far-distant home, he is doing the work of a chief pastor of the Church usefully, acceptably and hopefully. On accepting that bishopric he resigned the archdeaconry, the emoluments of which lapsed on his resignation. As the office is now one without either distinctive duties to discharge or emoluments to receive, I have resolved to hold it, at least for the present, myself, in preference to conferring it as a mere titular distinction. I could have wished that as the archdeaconry lapsed our legislature had made some provision, as they did when the Bishopric lapsed, for a clergyman who might on the one hand have been of material assistance to me in discharging the routine-work of the diocese as Chaplain, and at the same time have served as a supernumerary clergyman, to be employed at my discretion in supplying occasional vacancies in this island, which at present, owing to our

short-handedness as regards clergy, are provided for with
difficulty, and seldom satisfactorily.

Other vacancies have occurred among the clergy; two
veterans have retired from active service on their pensions;
three have died.   One of these is entitled to more than
a mere obituary notice.   The Reverend John Bradshaw
was one of those rare men who relinquished a profitable
secular calling for the comparative poverty of the sacred
ministry, avouching thereby his conviction that he was
" inwardly moved by the Holy Ghost to take upon him
that office and ministration."   To that sacred calling he
wholly gave himself during a long and faithful pastorate,
ministering alike to the bodily and spiritual distempers of
the poorer members of his flock.   Few men lived more
useful lives than he ; few of us shall carry to the grave
with us such sincere and heartfelt regrets as he did, alike
of high and low.

But though death has made hitherto such comparatively
small inroads on the ranks of my clergy, it has fallen to
my lot already to nominate to no less than six of the
eleven Barbados rectories, and to one of these twice.
This has arisen from the fact, that I have not hesitated to
move clergymen from rectory to rectory, where I deemed
the change might be beneficial to pastor or parish, or both.
For while, on the one hand, frequent changes and too
short incumbencies to allow of the man fully developing
his plans, and working out his system in practical detail,
are prejudicial to the welfare of a parish ; on the other
hand, change in a parish is often as salutary to vigorous
Church life as permanent fixity, even under a godly and
acceptable parish priest, "lest one good custom should
corrupt the world."   Three of the vacant rectories I have
filled, with the concurrence of the counsellors assigned me
by law, with clergymen who had done long and faithful service in the Windward Islands.   I know that such
appointments have not found favour generally with the
clergy of this island, and have been subject to some severe
criticism outside.   Let me once more justify the principle
which I have deliberately adopted, and to which I mean

in the main to adhere, though in the administration of
Church Patronage I decline to tie myself to any unbending
code. I consider it then most to the interest of Barbados
that those men should hold its most responsible positions
in the Church, who have given evidence by long, con-
tinuous (for this is the point) and successful service in the
unwieldy and most laborious charges in those islands, of
vigour, and tenacity of purpose in spite of hardships, disappointments and isolation, as well as of ministerial capacity and aptitude to deal with other men : while it is fair
that men who are willing continuously and uncomplain-
ingly to stick to work, which, if not always unattractive,
is always laborious and engrossing, and burdened with
many more cares and inconveniences than beset a clergyman in this more favoured island, should feel that in doing
so they are establishing a prior claim to positions here of
greater emolument and comfort. The mere fact of long
service in another island does not oblige me to move a
clergyman to a Barbados rectory, unless I judge him to
be personally fitted for it, but it does give him a claim to
be considered when it devolves on me to fill up such a
vacancy.

It has been alleged that in England it is not the rule to
look outside of a diocese to fill its more important cures.
I reply that, as a matter of fact, where considerations of
nepotism, or religious partisanship, or political necessities,
do not warp the selection of public patrons, (I say nothing
of private patronage,) those men are, as a matter of fact,
preferred to easier and more lucrative livings who have
shewn capacity after long service in laborious and unattractive cures. And I make bold to say that if this principle were more universally adopted, we should hear less of
the dearth of curates at home and of missionaries abroad.

It appears to me that there can be but two grounds for
promotion in the Church, as in every other service, se-
niority and selection. The former is far the easier : but
would it be cheerfully acquiesced in by the laity ? The
latter is a most invidious task for a bishop to be called on
to perform, especially in a colonial diocese, where he is on

a footing of more or less intimate and familiar intercourse with all his clergy, and where it is often most painful to him to pass over men whom he personally esteems and reveres, simply because he is bound to consider diocesan interests as more paramount than private feelings. I should be but too thankful to be divested to-morrow of the most disagreeable responsibility of patronage of all but purely honorary distinctions, if the Legislature of Barbados, and the Church Councils of the Windward Islands, would relieve me of it absolutely. As long as I am lawfully called on to exercise it, I must do it according to my conscience, and trust to the most favourable and charitable construction being put upon my motives.

While still upon the question of nomination to rectories, I wish to call attention to an act of the Legislature passed in 1876, to amend a clause in the Bishop of Barbados' appointment act, regulating the nomination to vacant rectories. The clause originally assigned as the bishop's counsellors the Rural Dean of the deanery in which the vacant parish was situate, its senior representative in the Assembly, and the senior member of Council resident in it, or, failing a resident member, the President of the Council. It so happened that then there was no President of the Council in the island, nor, in fact, is there such an official at the present time. The act to which I have referred substitutes the senior member of Council for the time being, i.e. either the General commanding the Forces, or the Colonial Secretary. Few who knew the late General commanding (Lieut.-Gen. Farren) as I did, could wish for a better and more faithful adviser. I, for my part, am more than content with his successor; but I do not hesitate to say, that the position in which this high military functionary is placed by this Act of Legislature is incongruous, and (I should think) distasteful to him, and it entirely nullifies what appears to have been the intention of the original act, viz., to protect the Bishop from possible mistakes in his appointments, by the more distinctly local knowledge

which his advisers, as therein constituted, could bring
to his aid.

Of other legislative acts during the period affecting
the Church, I need but mention with approval that under
which special intercession is now made in public worship
for the Governor and Legislature, the act adopting the
new Lectionary and shortened services, with other less important relaxations of the Act of Uniformity; the act
legalizing a Clergyman's renunciation of his clerical vocation, and freeing him from the disabilities attaching to
that station, and from penal consequences on embarking
in secular pursuits; and the act providing for a public
cemetery in St. Michael's parish. The passing of this
last-named measure has been a source of almost unmixed
satisfaction to me; the question, as you may remember,
was being agitated on my arrival in this diocese in
1873; I laid down in my Primary Charge the principles
on which, it seemed to me, it ought to be settled. Last
year I felt compelled—partly to avert a serious scandal
as to the burial of the dead in the monster parish of
St. Michael, after the closure of its churchyards by the
Board of Health, partly, too, to protect the present Rector
of St. Michael from what appeared to me to be an unjust attempt to force on him responsibilities which were
not fairly his, and to saddle his successors (as seemed
likely) with these in perpetuity—to undertake myself, with
some voluntary assistance from the Curate of St. Leonard's,
the burial of the dead in the new cemetery for five con-
secutive months. I consider that it was worth all the
trouble and discomfort which that somewhat incongruous
increase to my proper duties entailed, to have brought
about this satisfactory settlement, on the very lines within
which I hoped it would be settled; and I owe my best
thanks to the new Burial Board for having, in their first
appointment to the Chaplaincy, consulted my known wish
that it should be held by a clergyman not fettered by the
cure of souls in a district of the parish.

Though the labour was irksome, I do not regret the experience it gave me of burials, and their abuses as preva-

lent among us. The total disregard of punctuality, funerals often coming an hour or an hour and a-half after the time specified, sometimes arriving after my departure from the ground, when the shades of evening had already closed in, and made reading impossible; the heartlessness and indifference of surviving relatives, especially in the case of infants; frequently no one to take part in the service; the little coffin carried under the arm of some indifferent person, laid down by the grave and left; pauper funerals from the hospital or almshouses, consisting simply and solely of the parochial hearse, containing the grimly plain black wooden shell, with never a single mourner to follow the poor destitute to the grave: even when the regulation pair of mourners (insisted on in the cemetery rules) appeared, frequent unwillingness to alight from the cab and walk to the grave-side; and even in the case of large funerals, with all the adjuncts of banners and scarves (not always in entire harmony with the gravity of the time and place), only a few clustering round the grave to take part in that most solemn of all offices; the rest idly gossiping upon the paths or pastures in groups away, while the grave service was being read, after escorting the coffin to the grave-side.   These were some of my experiences as cemetery chaplain, and they forced upon me the conviction that we need much improvement in this respect at least. I cannot help feeling that our Burial Service, beautiful and most consolatory as it is to the true mourner, is pitched in too high a devotional key for all. It expresses aspirations which cannot be expressed without unreality bordering on hypocrisy, or at best an explaining away of terms, but over the grave of the consistent believer. We need an alternative service. I am fully alive to the difficulty, rather I should say the impossibility, of allowing the individual clergyman to determine which of the two he is warranted in using, according to his estimate of the character of the deceased. It appears to me, however, that the Church has provided a sufficient classification into communicants and non-communicants, the former being, as far as human

cognizance goes, in a higher spiritual state. I admit
that the criterion is more or less illusory (as all human
criteria are); there will always be communicants whose
spiritual state does not entitle them to that privilege,
and there are many estimable and amiable Christians
who, from some mistaken prejudice or other, have shrunk
from being communicants; but for practical purposes the
distinction is a real one, and sufficient to determine the
service to be used. The present office, which is essentially one of thanksgiving, is not a whit out of place
for the devout communicant, who has passed from behind
the veil to the more immediate fruition of the Saviour's
presence. An office of more sombre and penitential character, would be more in keeping with the Church's
attitude towards her non-communicant members. Be-
sides this, a short office for infants' funerals, and possibly
one for the unbaptized, would be desirable, with greater
choice as to the lesson to be read in the Burial Service.

Our circumstances here seem to call for radical changes
in regard of Marriage, as well as Burials. The statistics
with which you have furnished me in answer to my
Visitation Articles, shew that among us lawful marriage
is the exception, concubinage the rule: and the question
will fairly have to be looked in the face,—Is this state
of things compatible, or is it not, with the nominal profession of the Christian Religion? I am convinced that
no perceptible change for the better will take place until
the State in these West Indian Islands, and in particular
in Barbados—not in the interests of religion, but in its
own interests, to check the growth of pauperism—adopts
the principle of Roman law that *usus*, i.e. proved cohabi-
tation, constitutes legal matrimony. This practically is
(or was) the law in Scotland, where the public recognition of a woman as wife before witnesses, and the living
with her as such, constitutes a valid marriage. If the law
here saddled the man who was proved to have cohabited
with a woman for a given period, either continuously or
at intervals, with all conjugal and parental obligations,
one great obstacle to marriage would at once be broken
down, and less objection would be felt to contracting

matrimony in due legal or religious form. But there are other causes which prevent or delay the actual solemnization of marriage among our people, who yet live together, though unmarried, in fidelity and concord. Fashion with them necessitates a display both as regards apparel, equipage and festivity far beyond the couple's means; and, as we know, fashion is a tyrant to which wiser people than our simple peasantry think themselves forced to bow. Could not this difficulty be met by altering the law (which has been repealed in British Guiana), prohibiting marriages except between the hours of 8 and 12? Or might not clergymen be allowed (as, if I am rightly informed, dissenting ministers now do) to marry in private houses in the presence of competent, or (if it should be deemed desirable), of official witnesses, such marriages being duly registered as *marriages privately solemnized.* These would, in my opinion, be salutary changes, as facilitating the entrance lawfully on that estate which is now so generally enterprised—at least in the outset—illicitly; but even then, our circumstances here would necessitate some authorized relaxation as regards the use of the marriage service.

I could wish that the law empowering civil marriages, i.e. the entering upon legal matrimony without the customary religious service in church or chapel, were not, as it is, a dead letter; and I think it would be well that all ministers of religion should be *ex officio* civil marriage officers, i.e. empowered to unite parties in legal matrimony without the customary religious service in church. Surely such ratification of the civil contract alone would be more seemly, than the profanation (for I can call it nothing else) of the marriage service to cement an union which has been anticipated by the parties, it may be for years previously. At any rate, in such cases the clergyman ought to be authorized by law to use only the espousals, or nave service —the ratification in the face of the church of the marriage contract—and to omit the Benediction service in the chancel which follows it, commencing with the processional psalm, which surely should be reserved for those who enter on the marriage estate presumably pure.

In my Primary Charge I pointed out some abuses which had then struck me in the administration of the rite of Confirmation, viz. the extravagantly gay attire of the candidates, and the advanced age at which, on an average, they were presented, which was, as I then pointed out, wholly alien to the tenor and spirit of the Confirmation Office. Though the statistics of my confirmations for the last five years yield, on the whole, a lower average of age than the previous ones, yet I do not observe any marked difference in either respect. "De minimis non curat lex" is a sound maxim; but I doubt whether the question of the attire of Confirmation-candidates has not passed from the domain of taste into that of principle. The simple, untrimmed white dress, and a small plain cap, or coif, to cover the head (which seems to be almost of Scriptural obligation), are, no doubt, for girl - candidates, not only a becoming, but a symbolically instructive attire : for young and middle-aged women to deck themselves out in actual bridal attire, with a view to renouncing the pomp and vanity of the world, is not only contrary to good taste, but is gravely misleading to them. More than one of you have expressed to me your misgivings that the assumption of this attire is one among the unworthy motives which tend to swell our Confirmation-lists ; it is an excuse for extravagance, and sometimes (I speak from personal experience) for mendicancy ; and I have repeatedly had alleged as a reason why a day I had named for a Confirmation was unsuitable, the fact that the candidates could not be ready ; which did not mean that their instruction and spiritual preparation was incomplete, but that their finery was not yet procured and made up.

I suggest two remedies for this evil, on which I should like the opinion of my clerical ruri-decanal Chapters ; one, that the custom of the diocese be changed, which prescribes or encourages white dresses and veils for the female candidates, and that none, whether male or female, should be presented except in plain and sober-coloured ordinary Sunday attire ; the other, that Sunday Confirmations be discontinued, as attracting crowds, and ministering to that love of display which it is our duty gently, but firmly, to repress in our people.

With regard to the age of candidates, no doubt the average is a good deal raised by the few aged persons which still appear on almost every Confirmation-list ; but, even allowing for that, the bulk of candidates still consist of full-grown men and women. Now it is, I confess, a question with me — but one which I am not prepared dogmatically to answer—whether it is ever expedient to confirm persons very advanced in years. If it is, we need a fresh Confirmation Office for persons of mature age, for the present one is more or less incongruous. On one point, however, I am clear, that in the case of all, and more especially those of full age, an intelligent knowledge of the truths of the Christian religion, and more particularly of the obligations of the Confirmation promise, should be insisted on, save where the circumstances of the particular case call for exceptional treatment, as the absolute condition of admission to that rite. I am aware that this means reducing largely our communicant-lists ; but would that be a calamity ? Have we not many already on them who presumably are disqualified by ignorance from a real appreciation of the nature and sanctity of the Holy Eucharist ? You will not, I know, suspect me of ultra-Puritan leanings when I quote with approval from the topics of exhortation to communicants from the Westminster Directory of 1644 : " How necessary it is that we come unto Communion with *knowledge*, faith, repentance, love." And again, " The minister is to warn that they presume not to come to that holy Table, not only the scandalous and profane, but also the *ignorant*." It must surely be ignorance, or it would be profanity inconceivable, on the part of some of our communicants, which sometimes, after ministering the cup, leads one to regret that the mixed chalice has been declared illegal by the highest court of the Mother Church, not for doctrinal, or ritual, or antiquarian reasons, but simply because it might diminish the temptation, which seems to master some, to a greedy participation of its hallowed contents.

For this reason, I advise the use of lighter wines in preference to the more luscious in the Sacrament of the
Lord's Supper. The use even of real wine at all for this
purpose is far from being an universal custom of the
Catholic Church.

There is one point which must press heavily on you,
my reverend brethren, single-handed as you are almost to
a man, in connection with the celebration of the Holy
Communion, and that is the distribution of the elements
to each several communicant out of an average of 70,
100, or even over 200 (which some of you return), with
due obedience to the rubric which commands separate
distribution to each, with a somewhat long formula, the
result of a compromise between King Edward's two books.
I need not enumerate the many different expedients by
which this direction is commonly evaded by the over-
mastered clergyman, not only to spare himself, but to
avoid utterly wearying his congregation ; perhaps the
least objectionable of all is the widest departure from
both the letter and spirit of the rubric, viz. the recitation
of the formula for each kind to the entire railfull, and
then the silent distribution of the Bread and Wine to
each. Nor do I undertake to censure such evasions ;
but I point out that they are all opposed to the very
spirit and deliberate intention of the order. The question was raised at the last Revision, and the alteration
refused advisedly, on the ground that " it is the propriety
of Sacraments to make particular obsignation to each believer, and it is our visible profession that, by the grace
of God, Christ tasted death for every man." The relaxation I desire, to suit our special circumstances, is this,
that, where the priest is single-handed, or where the
number of communicants is very large, it should suffice
to recite aloud, before distribution, either for each railfull
or for the entire congregation of communicants, the present formulæ of administration in the plural number, and
then, in giving the bread and the cup to each, to say
simply, " The Body of our Lord Jesus Christ," " The
Blood of our Lord Jesus Christ" (which was the most

ancient form), or, as an alternative, "Christ died for thee," "Christ's Blood was shed for thee." These, however, are departures from the ritual order of the Church, which it must be for a Provincial Synod to approve, not for a single diocese to ordain at its discretion.

A Visitation Charge would be obviously incomplete without some reference to Education, and its prospects in the diocese. Referring to my Charge of 1874, I find that three of the points to which I then adverted on this head are now either accomplished facts, or are on the high-road to become so. Codrington College is now affiliated to the University of Durham, and I have already had the satisfaction of conferring (under commission from the Warden of that University) the B.A. degree on six Codringtonians, who have successfully passed the examinations for that degree ; and I learn that at the present time there are no less than fourteen men, including two old S. C. C.'s, up for the October, December, and January examinations.

The Education Commission sat, and sent in its report, and a well-considered and carefully-debated measure has been the substantial fruit of its labours. To the framer of that Act [c], who by his unwearied industry and tact steered it safe through all its parliamentary shoals and reefs, this colony lies under a deep obligation ; and his presence on the new Education Board is a guarantee that the beneficent intentions of the Legislature will be carefully worked out, in all the different departments of that many-sided subject.

By this Act, the Mission-house at Codrington College, with the consent of the S. P. G., will become a training-school for Elementary Teachers, and will exchange a condition of profitless vacuity for one of almost priceless utility to the cause of lower education in Barbados, and perhaps in our neighbour islands.

Two other successful efforts have been lately made towards improving Elementary Education : one has been

[c] J. W. Carrington, Esq., B.A., Solicitor-General, late member for St. James' parish.

the examination of selected children in our Church primary and infant schools in religious knowledge, under the auspices of the Church Council of Barbados, the report of which is already in your hands. As has been well remarked, if no other result of the deliberations of that body could be pointed to, it would have amply justified its *raison d'être.* I earnestly hope the plan so auspiciously initiated will be continued and extended ; and that upon examination of selected children, inspection of all schools in religious knowledge will be grafted.

The other effort has been the successful attempt to combine in an association, of which I have the honour to be President, the Public Elementary Teachers of the island of Barbados, for purposes of mutual discussion on topics pertaining to their profession, and on which their opinion is valuable and instructive. Hitherto their debates have been conducted with singular good sense, good temper, and ability. It so chances that on Monday next they will discuss the very question I propounded to you in my Primary Charge,—" How can payment of school fees and regularity of children's attendance be best enforced."

The project which was started some years ago, with fair prospect of success, of rebuilding St. Michael's Cathedral on a scale more suited to the importance of this colony, and the position which, happily, the Church holds in it as essentially the Church of the people, has had to be abandoned. It was well taken up by several non-resident proprietors, and by a few of our gentry here ; but it evidently did not, as I had hoped, grow in popular esteem, and the troubles of 1876 rather gave an excuse to, than caused the diminution of, interest in it. Comparatively little of the promised annual instalments were actually paid up, some promised subscriptions were withdrawn, and the tenders for the first section of the building (choir and transepts), in accordance with the excellent and original design of Mr. Oakley, the architect, were so extravagantly high, that the Committee have acted wisely in resolving to abandon the enterprise ; and, after deducting the expenses incurred in the preparation of the plans and

working-drawings, to return the money already contributed
to the Subscribers. The sister diocese will profit somewhat
by our loss, as some of the money that should have embellished St. Michael's Cathedral, Barbados, will go to
add a chancel to St. George's Cathedral in St. Vincent;
not such an one as we hoped for in this wealthier and
older diocese, but one more suited to the wants and
means of a disendowed diocese, where but little can be
afforded for the luxuries of religion. Some of our charitable institutions, notably the Goodridge Home, founded
by the munificence of a non-resident proprietor, but
hitherto unendowed, may fairly expect to attract to them
some of these liberated subscriptions : nor is it too much
to hope, that all the sums already paid in will be viewed
by their donors in the light of a deodand, once devoted
to sacred purposes, and no longer to be regarded as money
applicable to ordinary uses.

I have taken no steps towards giving effect to the sug-
gestions contained in my Primary Charge, as to collegi-
ating St. Michael's Cathedral Church, which is now simply
parochial, by engrafting upon it an honorary Chapter.
This is not because I am one whit less convinced of the
expediency of so doing, but because I have more and
more learned to recognize that some authoritative recognition of the respective rights and spheres of authority
and duty, of the parochial and capitular authorities severally, is absolutely indispensable as a preliminary step.

At present, although, through the courtesy and loyal
co-operation with me of the present Rector of the parish,
there exists a tacit *concordat* by which certain of the services
are recognized as parochial, regulated by him,—and others
distinctly cathedral, regulated by me,—there is nothing to
prevent a future Rector and Vestry of St. Michael's from
ignoring the Cathedral element altogether. The same is
true with regard to the seat-holders. They rent their seats
in the parish church of St. Michael's, and, as the law now
stands, are entitled to the use of these at every service
held in the church. As a matter of fact, their good feeling
(manifested in this and in many other matters) prevents

them from standing on their rights to the exclusion of the large congregations which frequent the strictly cathedral services, and they voluntarily waive undoubted rights, often, I feel sure, at the cost of some personal self-denial and inconvenience. But this position of sufferance ought not to be that which a Bishop should occupy in his Cathedral Church, and of itself makes the constitution of a capitular body inexpedient, till legislation has defined its status relatively to the parochial element. Obviously, the present is the best time for such legislation to be attempted, during the incumbency of a rector manifestly friendly to this co-ordination of the Parochial and Cathedral elements, and before the creation of vested rights in the person of a presumably younger man, who may succeed him when he vacates the rectory. How it may best be done is fairly a matter for discussion. Two modes suggest themselves to me, which may be worthy of your consideration. One is to regard the two elements as distinct, and to define by law their respective functions and their respective rights in the same building and its appurtenances, leaving it to the two bodies by mutual consent to work into each other's several systems, as much or as little as they like. The other is to attach the rectory of the Cathedral permanently to the bishopric, and, clubbing together the salaries of Rector and Curate, to place under the Bishop, as the actual workers of the parochial district, two Vicars or Residentiaries, with equal and co-ordinate rights and duties, at about £275 each. If this plan were adopted, it would become necessary to detach the Chairmanship of the vestry from the rectory, as it would be incompatible with the general duties of the Bishop : but this would be no revolutionary change, as the vestry is now virtually no longer an ecclesiastical body, but the civil incorporation or municipality of the City of Bridgetown and its suburbs, charged with almost wholly secular duties as to local government ; and it would be necessary to provide by law what has recently been tried by consent as an experiment, for the management of the monetary affairs of the Cathedral (exclusive of strictly fabric repairs) by a Committee of those who worship in it, and are presumably interested in its welfare.

Although, however, no change has been made in the constitution of the Cathedral as a Cathedral, much has been done and is being done to make it the centre of Diocesan life and work, thanks to the assiduous voluntary services of one of the masters at Harrison's College, and the unwearied efforts of a valued recruit from a sister profession. The choral services of the Cathedral have been maintained at a generally high standard of efficiency, with fair regularity of attendance and general decorum of behaviour, which would contrast most favourably with my earlier experiences of English Cathedrals: and the general attitude of the choir, both men and boys, in spite of many discouragements and repeated changes of their musical director, has proved to me that tenacity of purpose in a good cause, sound discipline, and unshaken loyalty to their leader in spite of ridicule and adverse pressure, may confidently be looked for from our people, though they move but in the humbler walks of life.

To improved choral services I may add the revival of Sunday Schools, and the making of a vigorous and persistent effort to bring religious teaching and religious influence to bear upon the young: and, as the natural corollary of Sunday Schools, children's services. To these we are simply feeling our way. Twice during this year, on Good Friday and Christmas-day in the afternoon, we have tried the experiment of gathering a multitude of little ones of all ages, ranks, and complexions within these spacious walls for an instruction-service, with happy and hopeful results, and we look forward to carrying them on more regularly after I have completed my visitation of the Windward Islands. We are also now ready for that department of work in a sea-port town which has been recognized as obligatory by the Church Council of Barbados, viz. ministrations to sailors in Carlisle Bay. The ship for this sacred purpose is now ready, and we only now wait for a sufficient force of Clergy willing to bear their share with us in this important missionary work.

But it is not at the Cathedral only that there has been a quickening of Church-life. All over this Diocese of Barbados churches have been improved, enlarged, and embellished, appliances for the more reverential performance of divine service provided, church music markedly improved. The general current has set, irrespective of party feeling (as it always should), in the direction of greater reverence in sacred things. St. James' parish church has been all but rebuilt, and is now one of the most church-like structures in the West Indies, as far as my experience extends; St. John's, St. Peter's, St. Silas' have added chancels; St. Ambrose, an aisle-gallery; St. Luke's, a sacrarium and organ-chamber; St. Lucy's, a bell; St. Thomas', a thorough internal renovation, in excellent taste and at considerable cost; St. Leonard's has added an organ-chamber, and has received many other appropriate and costly ornaments from some of those who worship there; St. Stephen's has been entirely renovated; to say nothing of minor alterations and embellishments: no fewer than twenty-three of you return alterations and additions, of more or less importance, to the fabric or ornaments as made in your several churches and chapels since March, 1874, the date of my last Visitation. All this implies interest on the part of clergy and laity in the outward decencies of Divine Service.

Turning from things outward to things inward, I have to thank by far the major part of my clergy for the general promptitude and accuracy of the returns made to my Visitation Articles. Some I have specially to thank for valuable, thoughtful and suggestive remarks upon the religious, moral and educational condition or wants of their district. On the other hand, the perfect accuracy of my generalizations is again marred, by a few needless omissions and palpable blunders on the part of some[d]; while my convenience in preparing this portion

---

[d] For example, one of the most populous districts in the heart of Bridgetown, returning its population as approximately 8,000, returns as the entire number of Baptisms during the past four years, 207. The next district to it, presumably equal in extent, returns 1,393.

of my Charge has been seriously interfered with by the
fact that several replies did not come to hand till after
the day specified,—the very latest I possibly could fix;
while three did; not find their way to me till the very day
before my Visitation, and one only came to hand late last
evening, after these pages had been written.

From a digest of these replies, it appears that out of
a Church-population of slightly over 144,000, at the cen-
sus of 1871,—now presumably considerably increased,—
there is an average of 11,874 at Sunday morning service,
and of nearly 10,000 at evening service, and about 4,000
communicants in average attendance at the Table of the
Lord: i.e. only 8 per cent. of the registered Church-population are in habitual attendance at church on the Lord's
Day morning, and only 2⅞ per cent. habitual Communicants: and yet, during the last five years, I have myself
confirmed 4,681 persons in this island alone. The statistics of marriages, burials, and baptisms tell their own
tale. During the four preceding years only 2,664 marriages are returned, as against 16,170 burials; while the
baptisms for the same period number 25,787, *of which
16,222 are registered as illegitimate, and only 9,565 as legitimate.*

At the conclusion of my Primary Charge, I deferred
anything like an exhaustive consideration of the moral
and spiritual condition of the diocese to some future occasion, as having then insufficient data on which to form
conclusions. It so happens, that the occasion has arisen
when I deemed it my duty to state my conclusions on
this subject, and I have learned with regret that I have
given wide-spread umbrage by doing so, and that my
conclusions have been deemed by some to be unjust as-
persions upon a fairly blameless community. No one
would be more thankful than myself, if those conclusions
could be refuted; but I venture to think that this will
not be successfully done by the *tu quoque* argument (however deserved), or by asserting (what no one doubted)
that vice is prevalent elsewhere.

On the present occasion, therefore, I prefer to quote on

this point the words of one of my own Rural Deans, on
whose calm judgment I place absolute reliance, who is
neither young, nor inexperienced, nor self-conceited, nor
unpatriotic: "There is still immense room for improvement in the religious, moral, and educational condition of
the people. Illegitimacy still abounds. In some instances the parents of illegitimate children, though unmarried, seem to live with each other faithfully; but
there is a great deal of illicit intercourse, and there are
many instances of polygamy. Falsehood, wrong-doing
of various kinds, and petty thieving,—the outcome of
poor corrupt human nature, — are everywhere com-
plained of."

I almost shrink from weakening the force of these plain,
sad words, by quoting from other clergymen's replies; but
"in the multitude of counsellors there is safety." Another
Rector writes, "Irreligion and immorality are very prevalent; many children are growing up without school-in-
struction or training." Another considers that "the religious and moral improvement is by no means on a par
with the intellectual." Another writes, "I have no reason
to regard with satisfaction the religious condition of my
district: the congregations are entirely out of proportion
to the population. Morally, there is no change; concubinage the rule, marriage the exception. Even the young
communicants fall into the prevailing evil habit of living
together before marriage; it falls like a blight on all our
young members." Another deplores that "marriages have
been but few, and most of them of persons already living in sin, or of persons who sought to cover their sin,
as proved afterwards. The difficulty with some is to
understand the marriage-vows, their meaning and importance, as shewn by the bad treatment and desertion
to which some wives are subjected." One more corrobo-
rative testimony to the truth of this sad bill of indict-
ment: "The standard and tone of the *religious* life of
the people greatly need improvement. The large majority of the inhabitants of the district absent themselves
from church all Sunday; in the evening, a few (compared

E

with the population) attend Divine Service. Not many
men, hardly any *young* men, are communicants. There
seems also to be very little knowledge of the Scriptures
among the people. The morality of the people generally
is also grievously low ; two-thirds of the births are illegitimate. A bluntness of the moral sense, absence of
proper public opinion, love of dress and show, insufficient
sleeping accommodation in the cottages of the labourers,
and habitual neglect of the means of grace, are among
the causes of the deplorable immorality that disgraces the
district. The returns of the police courts also point out
that much dishonesty, and violent conduct and language,
prevail among certain classes of the community."

Such, my reverend brethren, are some of the terrible
problems with which we have to deal in that state of life
to which it has pleased God to call us ; and when we
endeavour to call attention to them with a view to grap-
pling more earnestly with them, we may fairly expect
from our lay-brethren, not angry denunciation as traitors
and slanderers, but more earnest co-operation with us in
our efforts for the common good. But this, as a body,
they have hitherto withheld : all honour and thanks to
those, whether men or women, who have formed marked
exceptions to the general apathy.

One Rural Dean writes : "More workers in the way of
ministering to the religious wants of the people are needed.
I feel sadly my inability to cope single-handed with all
the work which is to be done. But how to obtain aid
in the work I know not ; I find my own time fully occupied in the routine-work of the parish."

A veteran town Curate, recognizes how much needs to
be done to improve the religious, moral, and educational
condition of the district, had he the strength and energy
of twenty-two years ago, when he first took charge of it,
or had he any lay-agency commensurate with the require-
ments of the case. A Curate in a laborious rural district
writes, "Lay help is sadly required ; I have not been able
as yet to find suitable district-visitors. There is not the
slightest help or co-operation afforded by the proprietors

and managers of the district (with a single exception), in anything that is required for the good of the people." And one of my elder brethren thus sums up his wants and discouragements: "There are, alas! other religious wants, such as a larger average congregation, both on Sundays and week-days, more prompt attention to the call to Confirmation, a larger and better Sunday-school, and some means of getting children in larger numbers to public worship. But these can only be supplied by a larger measure of God's blessing on ministerial effort, and by the gradual awakening of the laity to their religious duties, their share in Church-work."

I now commend to the careful consideration of all, the topics of this and of my previous Charge, for I have not thought it necessary to repeat much that was then said, and which still represents my unchanged convictions. And I do so in the earnest hope that it may please God to take away from us, as a community, all undue self-complacency, and all fallacious sense of security, and to enlist in a combined effort at better things all who love their country, and all who believe that Christianity is no mere form of sound words, but the power of God unto salvation.

Printed by James Parker and Co., Crown Yard, Oxford.